THE ADVENTURES OF
BLACK GOAT & YELLOW DOG

MEETING THE BEAR

Written by
Christine Odle

Illustrated by
Celeste Campbell

NEW YORK

LONDON • NASHVILLE • MELBOURNE • VANCOUVER

THE ADVENTURES OF BLACK GOAT AND YELLOW DOG
Meeting the Bear

Published in New York, New York, by Morgan James Publishing. Morgan James is a trademark of Morgan James, LLC. www.MorganJamesPublishing.com

A FREE ebook edition is available for you or a friend with the purchase of this print book.

CLEARLY SIGN YOUR NAME ABOVE

Instructions to claim your free ebook edition:
1. Visit MorganJamesBOGO.com
2. Sign your name CLEARLY in the space above
3. Complete the form and submit a photo of this entire page
4. You or your friend can download the ebook to your preferred device

ISBN 9781631953781 paperback
ISBN 9781631953798 eBook
Library of Congress Control Number:
2020921161

Illustration by:
Celeste Campbell

Cover and Interior Design by:
Rachel Lopez
www.r2cdesign.com

Morgan James is a proud partner of Habitat for Humanity Peninsula and Greater Williamsburg. Partners in building since 2006.

Get involved today! Visit
MorganJamesPublishing.com/giving-back

This Book Belongs To:

Dedicated to all our puppy dogs,

who have made our day-to-day lives so much better and are waiting for us at Rainbow Bridge.
Prince, Rascal, Sunny, Harlow, BJ,
Rexx, Daisy, Cali Bob, Thumper
and
Shadow

Thump
Thump
Thump

"What's going on out there?
It's too early to wake up an old yellow dog."

And then I heard that old familiar voice.

2

It sounded like a mouth full of marbles.
It was my old pal Black Goat. "Come out, I have neeews. Hurry, come out, I have neeews."

"Hold on to your Billy goat beard.
It takes a minute for an old yellow dog to get started first thing in the morning."
I crawled out of my dog house.
"OK, what's this all about?"

"I just heard that there is a bear down the block," replied Black Goat.

"A bear...?" I said. "Where in the world did you hear such a thing?"

"I was listening to that loud black-and-white bird, Maggie. She told her friends there was a bear living down the block," said Black Goat.

"Well, no wonder.
You know what a gossip Maggie is."

Black Goat stomped around in a circle. "I think we should go for a walk and see for ourselves."

"Maybe you should go for a walk.
Walking is hard on an old dog. And besides, have you ever seen a bear?"

"No, but I think it would be exciting!"

I took a deep breath and said, "Black Goat, you do know that bears eat goats, don't you? Hey, hey, where are you going?"

"To hide," Black Goat said as he ran away.

"Goats are so stupid!"

bear

bear

bear

5

Oh no, not again, I thought.

"Come out. We have to taaalk.
Come out. We have to taaalk."

"OK, OK, I'm coming. You don't want an old yellow dog to get his beauty sleep, do you? What do you want this time?"

Black Goat stood up tall and proud. "I think I need to face my fears and go see the bear. But, but, but will you come with me... please?" He said it with such a puppy-dog cuteness, how could I say no?

"OK, I'll go with you. But first, we should go see Burt the Badger."

Black Goat started shaking.

"I know he is gruff, but if anyone knows the truth about the bear, he will."

Burt lives in a hole 30 or 40 yards from our home. It didn't take long to get to his house, even for an old yellow dog. Before we could even knock, we heard,

"Who's there? What do you want? GO AWAY!"

I had to block Black Goat's escape to keep him from running away.

"Burt, it's me, Yellow Dog."

"Well, why didn't you just say so?" Burt said as he crawled out of his hole. "Oh, you're here, too, Black Goat," he snarled "What can I do for you, Yellow Dog?" In a low growl, he said,

"YOU keep quiet, Black Goat."

"Burt, it has come to our attention that there is a bear living down the block. Have you heard anything about this?"

"I have heard some rumblings, but I really don't know anything for sure. Why?"

"Well, Black Goat thinks he and I should walk down the block to see for ourselves."

Burt thought for a minute and then said, "You know that I'm not afraid of anything.

But even I would not like to have to tangle with a bear." And then he showed his very large teeth in an evil grin and said, "You know bears eat goats."

I turned to calm Black Goat down, and all I could see was a cloud of dust heading home. Here we go again. Goats are so stupid!

DAY 3

I didn't want to be awakened early, so I decided to get up and wait for the arrival of my old pal. I was not disappointed. He beat his head against my dog house. I wondered how many thumps it would take before he gave up. With each thump, he seemed to get more determined. He might have been getting angry.

"Excuse me," I said, a little too loudly. I thought Black Goat was going to jump right out of his Billy goat beard. After he calmed down, I asked what he wanted today. Black Goat said,

"After much thought and trembling, I
have decided that with or without you,
I am going down the block to see the bear."

"OK," I responded, "but if things look
dangerous, we will turn around and
come home." I was thinking that if a butterfly
landed on Black Goat's nose, we would be
running for home. "Do you agree?"

"Oh, yeees, yeees, yeees. Leeet's go!"

We began our long walk
down the block.

About halfway to the bear, we came upon Jerry Jackrabbit. This bunny has ears longer than the rest of his body but has always been a kind and generous animal.

"Hi, Jerry!" I shouted.

Jerry hopped right over to us. "Hey, it's great to see you, my friends! Where are you going on this fine day?"

"Jerry, we are on our way to see the bear."

"Yeees, yeees, the bear. Have you seen him, have you, Jerry?" exclaimed Black Goat.

By the look on Jerry's face, I wasn't sure what to expect.

Then, he said,
"Let me tell you a
story. Not long
ago, I made a trip
down the block to
find the special
green grasses
in the field. After
eating my fill,
I lay down in the
tall grass to take a nap. I was suddenly rousted
by a brown shape coming down on top of me
with this hot, hot,
breath flowing over my fur."

As Jerry spoke, it took all my strength to hold Black Goat from hightailing it back home.

Jerry continued, "I couldn't just lie there, so I jumped up and sprinted and zigzagged across the field. With every step, I felt something getting closer. All of a sudden, I heard a loud scream! My big ears are good for more than my great looks, you know. Whatever was chasing me just stopped! But not me. I ran and ran until I couldn't go any further.

Now, my friends, I don't know if this was
'the bear' but let me tell you, if it was,
it was fast! To be honest, it had really
hot, bad breath.
It was even worse than yours, Yellow Dog."

After that
comment, maybe
I'll bite off that
cute bunny tail,
I thought to
myself, not saying
anything.

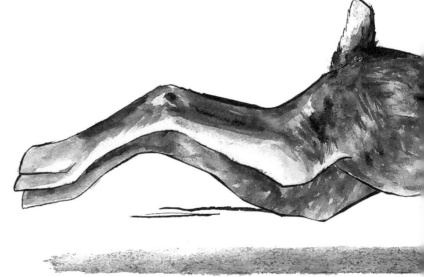

"Well, guys," Jerry said, "I've got to run,"
and he did.

Black Goat just stared after him. Then he said,
"You know how fast Jerry can run?
And the bear almost caught him?
We wouldn't stand a chance."

For once, I had to agree. "I think we should
walk back home and think about this."
We headed home.

DAY 4

All night, I thought and thought about what to do next. All I could come up with was that we had to finish what we started. I guess I wasn't the only one. As soon as Black Goat woke up, he was at my door. He didn't have to thump on my house. We just started back down the block together. We had just passed the place where we had talked to Jerry when we came upon Mr. and Mrs. Skinnybuck.

Mr. and Mrs. Skinnybuck are hard to talk to because they seem to always be on the move; very alert and jumpy. They just don't stay in one place too long. They approached us cautiously, and we started a conversation.

"Hello, my name is Yellow Dog, and this is Black Goat. We are walking down the block to see the bear."

"Bear, Bear? Where? Where?"

"I don't see a bear. I don't smell a bear. Where could he be?" cried Mr. Skinnybuck. "Be ready to run my love." And Mrs. Skinnybuck pranced like she was standing on hot coals.

"Whoa, whoa," I said. "The bear is on down the block. He's not here. Calm down." But they didn't, not really. "Do you have any information about the bear that lives down the block?"

Mrs. Skinnybuck replied, "At times, when we have been crossing along the back fence, we have heard this deep, low roar. We just ran for our lives."

Mr. Skinnybuck looked at us and said, "And that's what we're going to do now. If I were you, I would start back home now. It's going to rain. I wouldn't want to face the bear at all, let alone in the rain."

I'm an old yellow dog, and when it rains, my bones hurt. It's always better to be curled up in my bed when the rain comes. So Black Goat and I agreed to head home. Black Goat is also afraid of thunder. In Norwood, rain always comes with thunder. Goats are so stupid!

Once again, we set out after Black Goat came to get me. Maybe today would be the day. We walked for what seemed like miles. Soon, we came around a corner we had not seen before. Before we knew it, this large deer-looking creature came bounding up to us excitedly asking for help.

"Please, please.

My mother left me. I have been stuck in this field for almost a year. I just can't get out."

She was huge, and her legs were twice as long as Mrs. Skinnybuck's. So I asked, "Why don't you jump the fence?"

"Fence? Fence? What's a fence?" she exclaimed.

"Now, calm down, Miss, Miss... What is your name?"

"Elkie. My name is Miss Elkie."

In my long life, I have heard of an elk and may have seen one or two. They are always large and very mobile. Only the tallest and strongest of fences kept them from going where they want to go. So, what's wrong with Miss Elkie? She seemed tense. I spoke calmly. "A fence is that shiny thing that is held between sticks and goes around the field."

"Oh my, Oh my, Oh my.

Every time I get close to that thing, my whole body freezes. I can't do anything," cried Miss Elkie.

"Well," I said, "have you
looked for a gate?"

"Oh my, oh my, oh my.
What's a gate?"

Before I could
explain, she ran off in a huff. We didn't
have time to ask about the bear.

"Gee, was she silly?" Black Goat said.

Look who's talking, I thought.

DAY 4
PLUS 2
TOES

whatever
that is.

Today, I will talk to no one, including that stupid goat. I am going to see the bear no matter what! Black Goat must not have been out of bed yet, so I took off on my own. Too soon because as I was just getting out of the driveway, I heard this . . .

"Waaait, waaait!"

When I turned, I saw Black Goat running as fast as his short legs and fat belly would allow.

"You caaaann't go without me.
Who will protect you from the bear?"

"Who would indeed?
Well, come along then.
Time's a wastin'."

We set off again. After what seemed like hours, we came to a human's home that we had never seen before.

As we got closer, we heard that low, deep roar that Mr. and Mrs. Skinnybuck had told us about days ago. Fear turned us to stone. We just froze in our footsteps. Slowly, ever so slowly as an old yellow dog and a stupid goat could, we regained our courage. We moved like two ninjas around the corner of the house.

I kept smelling something that was familiar, yet different. Oh so slowly we peeked around the corner. There, curled up in a ball and behind a fence, was a big brown body . . . just like Jerry had described! Just when my thought was about to slip away . . .

Black Goat bellowed,

"wwwwhaaat's thaaat?"

As my sweat froze to my body, a commotion like I had never heard or seen before broke loose!

The big brown ball came to life! And the low,
deep roar became a deafening boom, and
at the same time, Black Goat fainted!
Stupid goat!

I ducked my head to show respect and perhaps save my life. I slowly asked,

"Please, Please

Mister Bear, we just wanted to meet you.
We don't mean any harm."

And then, to my surprise, the bear exclaimed,
"Bear? Bear? Where's a Mister Bear?"

"My humans call me Bear when I'm a little
excited. Mostly, they call me Baby Boo.
A real bear can be very scary. I know.
I saw one after we took a long drive in a truck
and then sat on the deck after supper."

I looked up. My eyes locked on to this large brown bundle of dog—a girl dog, too. She had breath like mine and a beautiful long tail with a white tip wagging so fast you could hardly see it. I leapt over to the fence in relief and joy. Then I was welcomed with three big, wet, sloppy kisses to my face.

The bear said, "So you're Yellow Dog, and that must be Black Goat. I was so hoping you would come to see me! Thank you, thank you, thank you! Thank you!"

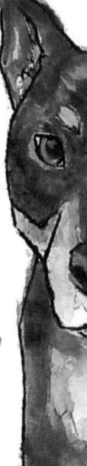

"Hey, Black Goat," Bear said, "wake up and join the party."

And you know, he did. We growled and ran up and down the fence for hours. Then we just sat and enjoyed being friends. I asked Bear how she had heard of us. She said the noisy black-and-white bird, Maggie, talked about us all the time.

Time passed, and too quickly, it was time to go home for the night. We said our goodbyes and promised to return soon.

On the way home, Black Goat was quiet. Finally, he spoke. "You know," he said, "we were really afraid, but we worked through it. We heard about the bear, and all we heard was bad. Then, we found out most of it was wrong. And we made a new friend! I think we've had a really good week."

Then he said, "It's great to have a friend like you, you know, to have these great adventures with and learn new things!"

I thought to myself, Maybe this goat might not be so stupid after all.

But I still think Miss Elkie is stupid.

About the Author

This is a story as told to **CHRISTINE ODLE**, the storyteller, by the animals in her neighborhood. She lives in the small town of Norwood, Colorado on a country dirt road with her husband—and at least two dogs—where each of the characters live. Each day she travels down the road, and when a character shows up she stops to have a chat. In each of the conversations, she imagines what they are saying back to her. As you,ll learn, even animals have a story to their lives (and, yes, Miss Elkie really lived in a field and would never jump the fence).

Christine grew up with over 100 stuffed animals in her room in the basement. It was there where she first learned to listen to those who really couldn't talk back in words, and where her imagination would take her on many adventures. One of her biggest real adventures was leaving home at the young age of 17 to attend College in southwest Colorado. She earned a couple of degrees and found her future world would be in the Wild West. She has since lived on an old-fashioned cattle ranch, owned a few businesses, written a business book called *Rockin, Your Business Finances*, is a paid speaker, and spends most of her time helping her clients find financial success. In her journeys and own adventures, she has found there can be many challenges and fears along the way, but if you face them head on (especially with your best friend), they can help you to succeed.

About the Illustrator

CELESTE CAMPBELL has been drawing since the time she first held a pencil. She has always loved using her imagination to explore new ideas and to create stories.

Celeste has a strong desire to illustrate many children's books. She has a firm belief that no one is required to completely grow up. Even as an adult, Celeste still looks forward to rainy days so she can stomp through the puddles and she loves to get together with friends and act out the scenes in children's books. She believes that earth life is here to teach us how to return to experience the full joys of childhood.

An experienced artist of 20 years, Celeste's artwork has a light and happy feel, unique to her style. Although she is an accomplished graphic artist, social media marketer and painter, her first love will always be childlike illustrations.

Celeste is the author and illustrator of *The Heart of a Knight*, her first published work. The book is the story of a lady knight who learns the lesson that friends are the most important gift of all.

Celeste currently lives in Saint George, Utah and is happily married.

A free ebook edition is available with the purchase of this book.

To claim your free ebook edition:

Visit MorganJamesBOGO.com
Sign your name CLEARLY in the space
Complete the form and submit a photo of the entire copyright page
You or your friend can download the ebook to your preferred device

Morgan James BOGO™

A **FREE** ebook edition is available for you or a friend with the purchase of this print book.

_____

CLEARLY SIGN YOUR NAME ABOVE

Instructions to claim your free ebook edition:
1. Visit MorganJamesBOGO.com
2. Sign your name CLEARLY in the space above
3. Complete the form and submit a photo of this entire page
4. You or your friend can download the ebook to your preferred device

Print & Digital Together Forever.

Snap a photo

Free ebook

Read anywhere

CPSIA information can be obtained
at www.ICGtesting.com
Printed in the USA
JSHW021459160821
17893JS00009B/251